The Story of Sir Dave

John Dougherty ■ Glen McBeth

The Legend of King Arthur

When good King Arthur ruled over Britain, he gathered together a company of knights. They were called the Knights of the Round Table. These brave men kept the kingdom safe from wickedness. They fought evil knights and rescued damsels in distress. Many tales are told of them and their courage.

Yet there are tales of the Round Table that remain untold.

Until now …

Chapter 1 – Sir Alric returns

A great feast had just begun at Camelot. Several evil knights shuffled into the Great Hall. They all looked rather embarrassed. Sir Alric followed behind, waving his sword about. He looked very pleased with himself.

This was because Sir Alric had actually defeated several *real* evil knights ... and this was quite unheard of. Sir Alric meant well but he often got things wrong. Once, King Arthur had sent him to rescue some damsels in distress. Sir Alric thought the king had said *animals* in distress. He had come back with a box of hedgehogs!

Another time, he'd spent a whole afternoon trying to get an empty suit of armour to fight him.

He wasn't even terribly good at feasting, to be honest. He kept poking himself in the eye with his spoon.

A hush fell in the Great Hall. The evil knights reluctantly made their way over to King Arthur and knelt before him.

"Now, evil knights," said Sir Alric sternly. "What do you want to say to the king?"

The evil knights looked at the floor. "We're very, very sorry," they mumbled. "We'll never ever do it again."

"You'll never do *what* again?" Sir Alric demanded.

"Be evil," said the evil knights, sheepishly.

"Good," said Sir Alric. "Now go and think about your behaviour."

King Arthur was both delighted and astonished. "Sir Alric!" he exclaimed. "How did you manage to defeat so many evil knights?"

Sir Alric smiled. "To be honest, Your Majesty, it's all thanks to my new friend, Dave."

"In fact, I was wondering," he continued. "Could you please make Dave a Knight of the Round Table?"

"Of course!" said King Arthur. "If this Dave fellow helped you to defeat all these evil knights, we'll be happy to have him! You have my word on that."

"Thanks!" said Sir Alric. He rushed to the door. "Dave!" he called. "*Da*-ave! Come in! The king says you can be a knight!"

All the Knights of the Round Table got ready to cheer their new comrade-in-arms.

Then Dave stepped in and everybody stared.

Nobody cheered.

Dave … was a chicken.

Chapter 2 – A problem

Sir Gawain leapt angrily to his feet. "Sire!" he said. "You can't knight a chicken! Camelot will be a laughing stock!"

"A laughing *chicken* stock!" sneered Sir Mordred.

"But you promised!" Sir Alric protested.

King Arthur turned pale. "I did, didn't I?" he said.

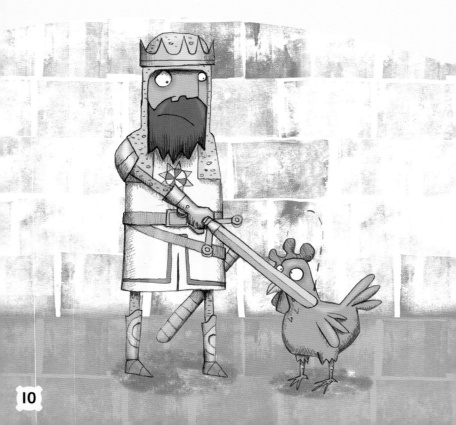

"Yes," agreed Queen Guinevere, worriedly. "You'll have to knight him."

"Alric – how exactly did Dave help you beat the evil knights?" King Arthur asked.

"They tripped over him," Sir Alric said, happily. "Then I bopped them on the heads and they dropped their swords. It was easy!"

"Oh," said King Arthur. He tapped his sword on Dave's shoulders (or the bit that probably counts as shoulders on a chicken). "Arise, Sir Dave," he said, gloomily.

"Buk-*awwwwk!*" said Dave and pecked at some crumbs on the floor.

The other knights were not happy about being joined by a chicken. Especially as Dave was, quite frankly, a rubbish knight. He didn't have any knightly manners. He didn't have any armour. He couldn't even hold a sword or a shield. Even worse, instead of saying "Sire" and "Verily, milord" (like knights are supposed to do) he only ever said:

"Buk-*awwwwk!*"

On the plus side, Sir Mordred kept tripping over him and bumping his nose.

Sir Mordred was sly and sneaky and nobody liked him very much. A bit of nose-bumping served him right, really.

So, after a while, the other knights began to think that perhaps a Chicken of the Round Table wasn't such a bad thing after all. In fact, they rather began to enjoy having Sir Dave around.

Chapter 3 – A terrible discovery

There was yet another feast at the castle. Everyone was having a jolly nice time.

"Hurrah for King Arthur!" shouted Sir Lancelot, raising a huge, silver goblet.

"Musicians! Play us a merry tune!" shouted Queen Guinevere, filling her plate.

"Ouch!" shouted Sir Alric, poking himself in the eye with his spoon.

"Buk-*awwwwk!*" squawked Sir Dave. He was flapping his wings. This was not unusual. Sir Dave often said "Buk-*awwwwk!*"

Then he said it again … and again … and again. Louder and louder each time. "Buk-*awwwwk!* Buk-*awwwwk!* Buk-*awwwwk!*"

The court fell silent and everyone stared.

Sir Dave let out one final, ear-splitting "Buk-*AWWWWK!!!!!!!!!*" Then he hopped out of his seat and pecked at some crumbs on the floor.

Just at that point, Sir Mordred came in. He went to the chair next to Sir Percivale.

"That's Sir Dave's seat," Sir Percivale said.

"Don't care!" Sir Mordred said, rudely. He sat down.

Immediately, he jumped up again.

"Eeeugh!" he said. "There's something soggy seeping through my armour!"

"Hmmm," said Sir Percivale. "There seem to be bits of eggshell all over your bottom."

Everyone began to laugh.

"Fools!" Sir Mordred hissed. "Don't you know what this means?"

"It means you've got an eggy bottom?" suggested Sir Lancelot. Everyone laughed again.

"No!" snapped Sir Mordred, purple with rage and embarrassment. "It means that *Sir Dave*, as you call him – *isn't* a 'him'. It's a 'her'!"

The other knights stopped laughing and went slightly pale.

"You mean that he's a *lady* chicken?" Sir Percivale asked.

"Of course he is!" said Sir Mordred. "Gentlemen chickens don't lay eggs!"

There was silence as King Arthur thought the matter through. "I'm afraid this changes everything," he said at last. "I mean – ladies can't be knights. That would be silly."

"You have to be brave and strong to be a knight," agreed Sir Gawain.

"I'm not quite sure how you un-knight somebody," said King Arthur. "Shall we just say that, since Dave is a lady chicken, he … er, *she,* can't have been a knight in the first place?"

"Good idea," agreed the other knights.

"Excuse me," said Queen Guinevere. "Are you saying that *chickens* can be knights, but *women* can't?"

"Well, yes," said King Arthur. "I mean, it was a bit silly having a knight who was a chicken. However, just imagine a lady being a knight! That would be ridiculous!"

"Ridiculous!" agreed the other knights and they all laughed.

"I see," said Queen Guinevere, icily.

If King Arthur hadn't been laughing so hard, he might have noticed that all the ladies of the court looked rather cross.

Chapter 4 – A mystery unfolds

The following morning, when King Arthur awoke, Queen Guinevere was nowhere to be seen.

"Perhaps she's downstairs, having breakfast," he said to himself. He went to find her but she was not there.

Oddly enough, the other ladies of the court had disappeared, too.

The Knights of the Round Table began to worry.

"Perhaps they've all been kidnapped!" suggested Sir Lancelot.

"We'd better go and rescue them," said King Arthur. "Men – get into your armour!"

That was when the knights discovered that their armour was missing, too.

"Oh no!" said King Arthur. "The ladies *and* our armour have been taken. We must save them. To our horses!"

"In our *underwear*?" asked Sir Mordred, horrified.

"Why, yes!" said King Arthur. "We're the Knights of the Round Table. We must be brave and fearless, even in our underpants!"

He ran outside and jumped on his horse.

"Hurrah for the Round Table!" yelled the other knights and they all ran after him. (It must be said that Sir Mordred did not yell very loudly or run very fast.)

Chapter 5 – The ladies go adventuring

The ladies of the court had not been kidnapped.

When King Arthur had knighted a chicken, they thought it was unfair. After all, he had never knighted a lady.

When King Arthur had de-knighted the chicken, they thought it was *incredibly* unfair. If gentlemen chickens could be knights, why couldn't lady chickens?

When King Arthur and the knights had laughed at the idea of ladies being knights, they had decided that enough was enough.

So they had got up *very* early. They had borrowed the knights' armour and Queen Guinevere had knighted them all. Since then, they had been having a lovely time riding around being knights.

First they'd gone questing. By mid-morning they'd already done half-a-dozen quests.

Then they'd had a jousting tournament. They'd all had a jolly time knocking each other off their horses.

Then they'd had a feast. Sir Enid and Sir Margaret had brought a picnic.

Now they were wondering what to do next.

"We ought to rescue a damsel in distress," said Sir Bronwen. "We haven't done that yet."

"I'm sure it's not just damsels who need rescuing," said Sir Guinevere.

"Buk-*awwwwk!*" said Sir Dave, pecking at a slug in the grass.

"Listen!" said Sir Matilda. "A cry for help!"

"To the rescue!" shouted Sir Guinevere. They all put on their helmets, leapt on to their horses and galloped off.

Soon, they saw a very strange sight. Riding very fast towards them was a man in his underwear. As he drew closer, they recognized him.

"Look!" said Sir Guinevere. "It's Sir Pantsalot. Er, I mean, Sir Lancelot."

"What could he be racing away from?" wondered Sir Isabella. "I didn't think anything scared him. Of all the Knights of the Round Table, he's the vest. Er, I mean, the best."

As Sir Lancelot reached them, he called out. "Knights, please help! King Arthur and his men have been captured by an evil baron!"

"Oh, dear!" said Sir Bronwen. "How evil, exactly?"

"Well," Sir Lancelot said. "His name is Sir Vicious. And he lives in Castle Terrible so I'm guessing he's *really* evil."

"Don't worry!" said Sir Guinevere. "We'll save them!"

Sir Lancelot looked at her suspiciously. "Are you sure you're real knights?" he said.

Inside her armour, Sir Guinevere smiled. "We're knights, all right," she said.

Chapter 6 – A dreadful battle

Sir Vicious and his men were holding King Arthur and his knights at swordpoint.

The ladies charged right into the middle of the enemy knights. Then there was a furious battle. People were bopping each other on the head and prodding each other in the tummy and knocking each other off their horses. It was all very fierce.

Meanwhile, King Arthur and his men stood to one side. They couldn't join in because Sir Vicious had taken their swords. Anyway, being in the middle of a fierce battle wearing just your underwear is terribly dangerous.

It wasn't long before Sir Percivale said, "Hang on! Isn't that our armour?"

King Arthur looked worried. "Do you realize what this means?" he said.

"Does it mean we've come to rescue ourselves?" asked Sir Alric. "There's me! I'm doing awfully well, aren't I?"

"That's not you, Alric," sighed Sir Gawain. "It's someone wearing your armour. I don't know who he is but he's got a ponytail tied with a pretty ribbon …"

Sir Percivale suddenly looked horrified. "It must be the ladies of the court!" he said. "They're fighting Sir Vicious and his men!"

"Don't be silly, Sir Percivale," said Sir Mordred crossly. "Ladies can't fight."

33

But the ladies *were* fighting. They were fighting as well as Sir Vicious and his men. In fact, it was beginning to look as if the battle might go on all day. Until …

"Stop!" yelled the tallest of the knights. Her voice was muffled by the armour. Everybody stopped. "I challenge Sir Vicious to single combat!"

"Good idea," snarled Sir Vicious. "This battle is taking too long and I want my dinner. The winner gets to keep King Underwear and his Knighties of the Washing Line."

Sir Vicious stepped forward. With one tremendous swing of his mighty sword, he knocked the knight's head clean off.

Chapter 7 – Horrifying happening

The Knights of the Round Table stared in horror. Knights weren't supposed to chop ladies' heads off. It wasn't polite.

Sir Vicious really didn't seem to care. "Mwahahahaha!" he laughed evilly and all his men joined in. "I win!"

For one terrible moment, it looked very much as though he had.

Then came a voice. "Not so quick!" it said.

"Who said that?" demanded Sir Vicious, looking round.

"I did," said the voice again. To Sir Vicious's horror, Sir Guinevere's body …

… began to get up.

The headless body stepped forward. On the ground, the helmet wriggled and then began to move.

Sir Vicious and his men stared. They were frozen with fear, as the helmet crept slowly along the ground. They shuddered. They shook. They whimpered with fright. They cried out in terror.

As the helmet reached the body, they lost any courage they had left. Screaming in panic, they leaped on to their horses. They charged back to Castle Terrible and slammed the drawbridge closed behind them. Then they all ran upstairs to their bedrooms, jumped into their beds and pulled the blankets over their heads.

"Hurrah!" shouted the lady knights.

King Arthur and his Knights of the Round Table stared in amazement. "How ... how did you do that?" Arthur asked. "He knocked your head off!"

"No, he didn't," said the headless knight. "You see, this armour's much too big for me. My head doesn't even reach the top, unless I stand on tiptoes!" A head popped out of the neck-hole. It was Sir Guinevere.

The knights cheered and danced with joy.

"What about the helmet?" King Arthur asked. "How did that move by itself?"

Sir Guinevere smiled again. "Easy," she said. "There was another knight in it." She bent down and picked the helmet up. Sure enough, underneath was another knight.

A knight who looked up at them and blinked.

"Buk-*awwwwk!*" she said.

Chapter 8 – All ends fairly

After that, King Arthur made a decision. He agreed that the ladies had earned the right to be knights. Not all of the gentlemen knights were happy about it. Glumly, they agreed to job share. The men got to be knights on Mondays, Wednesdays and Fridays. The ladies got to be knights on Tuesdays, Thursdays and Saturdays. On Sundays, everybody feasted.

At least, that's how it was at first. However, after a while it began to feel a bit silly being knights on separate days. Soon, they all started to be knights at the same time. Before long, nobody talked of lady knights or gentlemen knights. All of them, men and women, were Knights of the Round Table.

King Arthur never knighted another chicken but Sir Dave remained a knight. When Guinevere went out questing or jousting, Sir Dave rode with her, perched on the front of her saddle.

So everybody was happy.

Well – nearly everybody. Sir Mordred never quite got over being rescued by the lady knights. It wasn't just that. Several of them turned out to be braver and cleverer. They were just generally better at being a knight than he was. This made him really cross.

So cross that, many years later, Sir Mordred stole all the books that had been written about the Knights of the Round Table. He took out the ones about the lady knights – including the story of Sir Dave – and buried them. That is why nobody knows about them.